These common sayings spring from the ancient traditions of meditation and calm attentiveness found in Zen Buddhism. Paired with selected paintings from Jon J Muth's five award-winning "Zen" books, these twelve simple meditations may help you discover an intuitive path to your own happiness!

Library of Congress Cataloging-in-Publication Data available

ISBN 978-1-338-34602-2

10 9 8 7 6 5 4 3 2 1   19 20 21 22 23

Printed in China   62

First edition, April 2019

Book design by Charles Kreloff and David Saylor

Zen
Happiness

WITH ARTWORK BY

Jon J Muth

SCHOLASTIC PRESS / NEW YORK

We are born again with each new day.

Words,
both true and kind,
can change the
world.

Be someone you want to be around.

What we do now is what matters most.

What we think,
we can become.

With our thoughts,
we create the world.

When you reach the

op, keep climbing.

Be kind to yourself. Whatever you do today, let it be enough.

remain hidden:

and the truth.

You, as much as anyone in the universe, deserve your love and respect.

From stillness,
life rises.

May all beings have happy minds.